SUBWAY SURFERS

OFFICIAL GAME GUIDE

Scholastic Inc.

CONTENTS

TM & © 2021 Sybo ApS.

ISBN 978-1-338-76087-3
10 9 8 7 6 5 4 3 2 1   21 22 23 24 25
Printed in the U.S.A.   40
First printing 2021

Written and designed by Dynamo limited

Thanks to Adam Collier, Naz Cuevas, Jonas Georgakakis, Bodie Jahn-Mulliner, Trym Johansen, and Sylvester Rishoj

WELCOME TO THE WORLD OF SUBWAY SURFERS

Subway Surfers is an endless runner, or infinite runner—a type of mobile game that generates a never-ending world to run through while the player has to rack up the highest score they can without crashing!

POGO STICK

SPRAY CAN

Endless runner–style games date back to the 1980s. But they became especially popular when mobile games took off. They're perfect as a digital snack to pick up on the go, or as a longer playing session given the World Tour mechanic that *Subway Surfers* has!

Iin 2008, Danish CGI artists Sylvester Rishøj and Bodie Jahn-Mulliner made a short animation about a young graffiti artist escaping from a security guard and his dog. They later founded a studio called SYBO Games, but it wasn't until they thought about making an endless runner that they found the perfect combination of gameplay and theme. "As soon as we had the concept nailed, everything sort of just fell in place," says Rishøj.

DID YOU KNOW?

Subway Surfers was released in 2012 and became the most downloaded mobile game of the decade, now with 3 billion downloads and counting!

MEET THE CREW!

JET PACK

5

PLAYING THE GAME

In *Subways Surfers*, you run along the subway tracks, dodging trains and other obstacles while you collect coins, keys, power-ups, and other items, and try to build a high score!

COINS AND KEYS

Coins and keys are used to unlock characters and hoverboards. Coins are common, but you need a lot of them to unlock most things. Keys are much rarer!

ALL NEW

Each edition lasts about a month and has its own characters and boards. We've covered as many as we can in this book, but there are many more!

JINGLES

LOCATION, LOCATION, LOCATION

Each edition also has a collectable item related to that location—pick these up to unlock season rewards!

GREECE

SHANGHAI

HOVER-UP

The most useful power-up in the game is the hoverboard. Once collected, you can activate it at any time by double-tapping the screen—and for a limited time, you'll be able to survive any crash!

YUTANI'S GREATEST INVENTION

TAKE NOTE

As you play the game, you'll see similar patterns of obstacles come up—each run is randomly generated from these smaller sections. If you can remember how each pattern works, you'll be better prepared.

UP AND OVER

If you spot a section coming up that you know is tricky, activate a hoverboard if you have one! Don't wait until you're in trouble— it'll be too late.

SAFE PATH

If you're struggling to see the safe path, look out for coins. The game never puts coins in impossible places to fool you, although some need power-ups to reach!

CHECK ME OUT

And don't forget to check the "Me" screen regularly—limited characters from previous editions are often briefly available again, so don't miss them!

STAR
HEADPHONES

HOVERBOARD

Jake

The first character you meet in *Subway Surfers* is the group's leader!

Jacob "Jake" Bressler is a charmer and a risk-taker with a passion for skating, travel, adventure . . . and food. Especially junk food! Jake's detailed knowledge of his home city, combined with his careless attitude toward rules and authority, led him to explore the city's hidden and dangerous spaces—and develop the urban activity known as subway surfing.

SWEET STYLE

Jake's look is Classic street style with a cap, hoodie, jeans, and sneakers. His other style options were both introduced in the Miami update of the game. They include his Dark outfit, which is great for sneaking through shadowy tunnels . . . And then there's the old-school vibes of his Star outfit, for when you don't care who sees you. Sweet bling, Jake!

 CLASSIC   **DARK**   **STAR**

Though Jake is an intelligent kid, he's only an average student—he's too much of a dreamer to focus on schoolwork. He has a head full of ideas, some of them more sensible than others . . .

THRILL SEEKER

Jake always has to go further than anyone else, which can lead him to overreach, even with his keen skating skills. He finds it hard to turn down a bet or a dare! When Yutani discovered the alien technology that created hoverboards, with their ability to glide across surfaces skateboards can't cope with, he couldn't resist. He was the first to try it out . . . and the first to crash it!

Jake can be a little insensitive to his buddies' problems, especially when he gets absorbed in his own pursuit of thrills and adventure. But he's a loyal friend who'll take risks for others, as well as just for fun.

DID YOU KNOW?

Jake's tagging alias is JaZe. (This can be seen in the first scene of the animated series!)

HOLIDAY LOOKS

Jake has also had limited-edition holiday variants!

Zombie Jake was released for the 2012 Halloween update and has been brought back several times for the New Orleans, Transylvania, and Mexico updates.

Festive Jake was released for the St. Petersburg update of Christmas 2020.

ZOMBIE JAKE

WHO IS THIS FESTIVE RABBIT?

FESTIVE JAKE

COPENHAGEN

The birthplace of *Subway Surfers* . . .

Copenhagen didn't make its debut until the fifth anniversary of *Subway Surfers* in May 2017, but it has a special place in the game's history. SYBO and KILOO, the companies that co-developed *Subway Surfers*, are both based in Denmark—and SYBO's headquarters is in the country's capital, Copenhagen.

This city on the coast is famed for its canals and handsome and colorful waterside buildings, which make up the backdrop of this edition.

Copenhagen is home to Tivoli, one of the oldest theme parks in the world! It has a wooden roller coaster that's over a hundred years old—not sure I'm brave enough to ride it, but Jake's ready to try . . .

MEET THE LOCALS

The Copenhagen update introduced Freya. In her first style, she's an opera singer with a rock 'n' roll edge. Check out that leather jacket and ripped jeans!

Her second style casts her as a Viking, with a winged helmet and braided hair.

CHUNKY VIKING BOOTS

HITTING ALL THE RIGHT NOTES

HAMMER BOARD

HOP ABOARD!

In keeping with the Viking theme, the main board for Copenhagen, is the Hammer board. Major Thor vibes!

However, to tie in with the fifth anniversary of *Subway Surfers*, an additional board was introduced—the Birthday board! Not hard to guess what this gift is when it's wrapped up.

AMSTERDAM

The chill-out capital of the world!

Amsterdam was the first edition of the 2017 tour. The capital of the Netherlands has a beautiful canal network at its center, and the landscape outside the city is also famous for its flowers (especially tulips) and windmills.

You may also have spotted a waffle stand while playing this edition—the *stroopwafel* is a type of cookie with caramel sandwiched between two thin waffles, and it is a Dutch speciality! The city also has the best pancake houses anywhere in the world (sorry, Paris)!

One of the best soccer players of all time, Johan Cruyff, was born in Amsterdam. He played for the city's biggest club, Ajax. With him as captain, they won the European Cup three times in a row!

JOLI GOOD

Amsterdam's native character is Jolien, a cool city girl with purple and blue hair. In the original edition, the alternative outfit dressed her as a florist to reflect the Netherlands' flower trade. She had gardening gloves and tools . . .

whereas the second edition offered players the Spring outfit with a yellow overcoat.

SPRING SURPRISE!

KNEE PROTECTION FOR SKATING

PEDAL BOARD

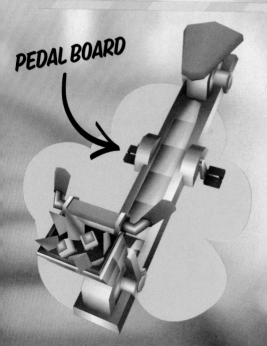

FLOWER POWER

The board for Amsterdam is Pedal. It's designed like a florist's bike with a basket of flowers on the front. The only difference is that you still ride it like a board, not a bike, which is confusing. But at least the seat on the back gives you somewhere to sit down when you're not skating!

I GOTTA ADMIT, THAT MY BALLET TRAINING COMES IN HANDY WHEN I'M JUMPING OBSTACLES IN THE TUNNELS! BUT I HAVE TO BE CAREFUL NOT TO TWIST AN ANKLE—MY TEACHER AND MY PARENTS WOULD KILL ME . . .

COLLECT HATS TO UNLOCK TRICKY!

SHE'S FAMILIAR WITH COINS . . .

Tricky

Meet the gang's rebel girl—and dance diva!

Tricky's a complicated character. She's incredibly smart and her parents are rich . . . but they don't know she has a hidden passion for skating, tagging, and hanging out in tunnels with her friends.

Tricky is the first character you unlock in the game—you only need three hat tokens, which are easy to pick up. Her basic outfit is a red hat, white tank top, and baggy jeans. But there's also her camo outfit,

ALTERNA TRICKYS

The classic hip-hop stylings of Tricky's Heart outfit is the only time she appears without glasses. Let's hope she's got her contact lenses in, or she might miss a few jumps!

Several Christmas-themed editions have featured Elf Tricky, who comes in three outfits—the basic Elf costume, the Ice version (which is cool!), and the Candy outfit.

HEART

CLASSIC ELF

ICE

YOU'LL NEVER SEE HER COMING!

which won't help her blend in much in a city, but it looks pretty sweet. And all those pockets in her cargo pants mean she can carry plenty of spray cans, coins, and keys!

DOUBLE LIFE

Tricky's parents want her to focus on schoolwork and ballet. She's enrolled in the elite Boshkin Ballet School, but she secretly wants to be a street dancer.

Her family has no idea she leads a double life as a skater. She doesn't even let them see her in her skating clothes—she gets changed after leaving the house before going to hang with her friends! Yep, there's a reason why you can't unlock a ballet outfit for Tricky—she'd never go skating in her tutu.

HEIR STYLE

She's an only child, which means Tricky is the sole heir to her family's huge fortune. With all that money she can do anything she wants . . . as long as her parents approve.

They certainly don't approve of her getting into trouble—so she really can't afford to get caught! If the guard reports her activities to her parents, it could spell the end of her subway surfing days.

Tricky takes skating seriously—when working on a new trick, she'll calculate the angles and take the physics of movement into account. She's a real perfectionist, and gets frustrated if she fails to get her tricks and break-dancing moves just right.

MATHEMATICAL ACROBATICALS

Tricky

LONDON

Just the place for your Christmas shopping!

The capital of England always appears as a Christmas stage, making its debut in 2013. This makes sense because one of the most famous stories about Christmas is *A Christmas Carol* by Charles Dickens, and it's set in London.

London had to feature in *Subway Surfers*—its subway system (the London Underground) is the oldest in the world! The line from Paddington to Farringdon was opened in 1863, and is still part of the network today.

In 2012, London became the first city to host the Summer Olympic Games three times!

LONDON LAD

London is one of the few locations with more than one character. Its original release includes Jamie, a sporty-casual lad . . .

In the 2018 re-release, his alternative outfit styled him as a Victorian gentleman with a top hat.

But the 2014 edition also offered Buddy! Unlike most snowmen, this little dude has legs, so he can ride a board . . .

OLD-SCHOOL CAMERA

MODERN CAMERA

JINGLE BOARDS!

Three Christmassy boards have appeared in London: Snowflake, Jingles, and Rudy.

RUDY

SNOWFLAKE

JINGLES

EDINBURGH

Pull off some killer moves in your kilt!

The world's biggest performing arts festival is the Edinburgh Festival Fringe. It has over 50,000 performers every year—from comedians and musicians to actors and acrobats. Maybe one day I'll get to dance there!

Edinburgh first appeared in July 2020. The capital of Scotland is built on steep slopes, which means its buildings are almost stacked up on one another in some places. It's also known for having an amazing castle!

LO-CAL

Edinburgh's character is Callum, who merges traditional Scottish dress with punk style! His kilt and sporran really work with his boots and leather jacket. A safety pin through his ear completes the look.

The alternative outfit turns Callum into a changeling! These creatures appear in folklore all over Europe, including around the border between Scotland and England. The myth was that fairies or elves might steal a baby and replace it with one of their own in disguise . . .

PUNK IN THE TRUNK

PUNK BOARD

Edinburgh also offered the Punk board. This hoverboard doesn't just look punk, it actually has the word PUNK actually written on it. Those spikes should make sure no one gets in your way!

I LIVE MY LIFE BY THE FIVE ELEMENTS OF HIP-HOP: MC'ING, DJING, BREAK DANCING, GRAFFITI, AND EDUCATION! OK, AND SKATING. IS THERE ROOM FOR A SIXTH ELEMENT? WHO DECIDES THIS STUFF?

GOLD VINYL FOR GOLD SOUNDS!

Fresh

Fresh was born in the wrong time: His head is totally in the 1980s.

Fresh wears his hair in a hi-top fade—the classic hip-hop haircut! His default outfit is a green tank top, red shorts, and sneakers ... His awesome square glasses are totally geek chic, too!

It may be called the Funk outfit, but this Fresh ensemble is way more De La Soul than it is Earth, Wind & Fire. Note the retro boom box—beats listening to tunes through a phone speaker!

GOOD SPORT

The Sport outfit sees Fresh ready
to hit the basketball court! This is
the one time you'll see him without
his boom box, because you can't play
basketball without a basketball.
Also the boom box would kind
of cramp his game . . .

KING OF
THE COURT!

SONIC
BOOM BOX

OLD-SCHOOL COOL

Fresh lives and breathes 1980s fashion, music, and lifestyle. It was the era when tagging really took off, and he knows it inside out.

He can usually be seen carrying his boom box, which he calls Boomy—he even carries it while skating! He uses Boomy to make his own music, too.

DID YOU KNOW?

Fresh's big sister, Ella, has also appeared as an unlockable character in the game. She has three outfits of her own!

FRESH

WISE GUY

Fresh is the most levelheaded of the gang—good at defusing arguments and keeping them all together. He thinks before he speaks, which is more than you can say for Jake!

BRINGING THE BEATS!

His family is close-knit, but they can be a bit stifling. In a sense, he and Tricky are pretty much opposites! But Fresh values being able to get away from his family and explore the city just as much as Tricky does.

WELL-RED!

ICELAND

The most aptly named country in the world!

One of the world's coldest countries, Iceland first appeared in *Subway Surfers* in September 2016. The whole country has a smaller population than most of the cities featured in this book!

Iceland is also known for its active volcanoes—that's what makes it the Land of Fire and Ice. You may have noticed volcanoes in the background of this edition . . . If you stand at a safe distance, you can cook food on the hot rocks, without the hassle of lighting a barbecue!

Iceland may be covered in snow, but it's also one of the greenest countries in the world—it runs almost completely on renewable energy. That's what I call smart living!

WOOLLY IDEA

Iceland's character is Bjarki, who comes dressed for the climate in a thick sweater. He also carries . . . a sheep? Hey, all the cool kids these days are carrying a sheep.

SHEEPISH EXPRESSION

Bjarki's Power outfit has echoes of the country's soccer uniform, with its red Viking helmet on the vest. Not as warm, but you can always plunge your hands into the sheep's wool if they get cold. Finally, the Fisher outfit! Fishing is one of Iceland's biggest industries.

POWER STANCE

BLUE BOARD

The board for Iceland is Big Blue—a hoverboard that looks like a shark. Fermented shark, or hákarl, is an Icelandic national dish! It has a very strong smell and tastes very, very fishy, but apparently it's tasty . . . once you get used to it!

BIG BLUE

PARIS

You can go in-Seine here!

One of the most-visited locations in *Subway Surfers*, the French capital was the first place to feature in the game five times! It debuted in June 2013.

Paris is a world center for art, fashion, and learning, and is known for its street cafés, which you can see in the Paris edition of the game. You can also see the city's most famous landmark, the Eiffel Tower, in the background. It stands on the bank of the Seine River. The subway's entrances are very distinctive, in a style called Art Deco!

Paris has some of the greatest art galleries in the world, including the Louvre, where the *Mona Lisa* hangs! I still say they need some examples of great street art, though . . .

MIME TIME

The unlockable character in Paris is Coco. Her standard outfit—striped T-shirt, beret, and face paint—is what mime artists traditionally wear. (Mime artists are performers who don't speak, and pretend stuff is there when it's not . . . it's kind of a French thing, though it was invented by the ancient Greeks!)

You can also unlock the Art outfit, where Coco wears a painter's smock (but still has the mime makeup).

SMOCK AND ROLL

SHHHHH!

FLOWER POWER

ROSE

The hoverboard for Paris is Rose—appropriate for the world's most romantic city! The background is the French flag, known as the tricolor—red, white, and blue. Lots of other countries have copied this combination of colors, but France was one of the first!

CHECK OUT THAT MOHAWK!

SPIKE'S GUITAR

SPIKE

Keeping it real!

Punk's not dead when Spike's around! He can be unlocked by collecting guitars. The "A" on his back stands for anarchy—living without rules! (Although you still

PUNK MALE

Spike's standard outfit is the kind of classic punk look you'd see in New York or London in the 1970s—Mohawk hairstyle, sleeveless black jacket, and gray T-shirt . . . Those big black boots are ideal for jumping up and down at a concert—maybe not so great for skating, though!

SUPER-SKINNY JEANS

The Rock outfit is a modern, metal style with eye makeup and spiked wristbands . . . Whereas his Punk look is more of a Californian punk style—spiked green hair and a striped tie (but no collar). The great thing about this look is you can just raid your dad's wardrobe for a tie!

have to play by the rules of the game when you play as him.) He also has the awesome ability to change his hairstyle along with his outfit!

MONACO

Hanging with the jet set!

One of the world's richest and most glamorous places, Monaco featured in the March 2017 and May 2018 editions of the game. It's a microstate—a country in its own right on the south coast of France.

Monaco is the second-smallest country in the world after Vatican City. It's where the wealthy go to moor their yachts and sit in the sun. Its glorious coastline is a feature of this edition. It's also known for its casinos—just as well, there are plenty of coins lying around . . .

More than 30 percent of the population of Monaco are millionaires! My parents sometimes talk about moving there, but I don't think I'd fit in—and I'd miss my friends too much . . .

BOY RACER

Monaco's character is Philip—a rich kid with a sporty style and a love of tennis. His first alternative outfit is the Racing outfit—reflecting the famous Monaco Grand Prix, which is one of the only Formula One races to take place on public streets rather than a racetrack! It can get pretty chaotic . . .

PERFECT SERVICE

TROPHY WINNER!

And then there's the Captain outfit (perfect for sailing!) with a hat and telescope. Not sure we'd take orders from him, though!

NEED FOR SPEED

SPEED DEMON

In another nod to Formula One, the Monaco board is the Speeder, which is shaped like a racing car. Its colors are the same as those used by Ferrari—the oldest and most successful team in Formula One, which has won the Monaco Grand Prix ten times!

ZÜRICH

This city runs like clockwork!

The capital of Switzerland first appeared in the game in April 2019. One of the world's most scenic cities, it's right next to Lake Zürich and the Alps.

It's pretty small, but is rated as having the highest quality of life of any city—if you can afford to live there! Zürich is also good if you want to go skiing—look out for the cable cars in the sky while you're playing . . . This edition also introduced Rabbot, the pink robot rabbit character!

For several centuries, Zürich was a city-state with fortified walls—basically it was one huge fortress! It's a shame they tore the walls down in the 19th century. If they were still there, I'd tag them . . .

HUGO FIRST

Hugo is your unlockable dude for Zürich. Switzerland is famed for making clocks and watches, and Hugo's helmet has a watchmaker's eyeglasses on it—the lenses are for magnifying the tiny cogs when you're trying to get them into place, or fix them when they're broken.

WATCHFUL EYES

Hugo's first alternative outfit, the Mountain outfit, is a traditional Alpine costume . . .

And his Pirate outfit is totally steampunk, with watch parts and tools and a robot parrot.

TIMELESS STYLE

CLOCKWORK HOVERBOARD

TIME TRAVEL

The Clockwork hoverboard continues the clock theme, with cogs and a classy wood finish. The timing of all your jumps will be perfect with this!

(DISCLAIMER: Timing of jumps cannot be guaranteed. The manufacturer accepts no responsibility for injury or capture by the guard.)

> *WHATEVER MY HOME PLANET IS LIKE, I HOPE IT HAS LOWER GRAVITY THAN EARTH—IMAGINE THE JUMPS AND TRICKS YOU COULD PULL OFF! AND IT'D HURT LESS WHEN YOU FELL, TOO.*

COLLECT UFOS TO UNLOCK YUTANI!!

YUTANI

The gang's resident tech genius, whose inventions are out of this world!

For a long time, we didn't know much about Yutani! She spent all her time in her alien suit, but recently she's come out of her shell . . . literally. Unlike other core characters, Yutani has just two outfits. Her default outfit is her alien suit, which has four arms.

UNSUITED

In 2019, Yutani was finally given a second outfit with the Houston edition, and we learned what her hair looks like! She has a Ghostbusters-style backpack with mechanical arms, so this time her extra limbs are especially handy! That's how Yutani thinks—there's always a tech-based solution to any problem . . .

Yutani is the hardest token character to unlock. You need 500 of her UFOs to get her, which means some serious grinding!

Which of those arms are her real ones? We're not totally sure!

OUT OF THIS WORLD

Yutani is adopted and none of her birth records exist—which is why she wonders whether she was born on Earth at all . . .

She's the youngest member of the gang, but has achieved more than any of them. Her love of design and invention means that she holds three registered software patents.

GREEN MACHINE

LIVE WIRE

Yutani's the one who invented the hoverboard, using a piece of alien anti-gravity technology she found. The fact that she was able to understand and use it might be evidence of her genius, or her alien origins . . . or both!

The gang have managed to keep their hoverboard technology a secret for now—it gives them the edge over the subway guards! However, Yutani is also a keen vlogger (her weekly live show streams on Yu Tube) and, in her enthusiasm, sometimes says too much.

FESTIVE YUTANI

YUTANI

LIVE WIRE

VENICE

Surfing in a city on the water!

This old Italian city stands in a shallow bay and has no roads, just canals! It first appeared in *Subway Surfers* in June 2015.

Venice was once one of the most important trading posts in the world, selling goods between Europe and Asia, but today it's mostly a tourist town. At the edges of the gameplay area, you can see the distinctive boats known as gondolas, which are used to punt up and down the canals.

Venice is built on a group of 118 small islands connected by over 400 bridges! But don't confuse it with Venice Beach, which is in California and has also been a World Tour stage . . .

BOAT BOY

Venice's character is Marco, a young gondolier. His default outfit is in the traditional gondolier's style . . . His first alternative is the Mask outfit.

COOL HAT!

Venice was once famous for its masked balls, where partygoers would dress up and hide their identities.

The name Marco comes from the famous Venetian merchant and explorer Marco Polo, who wrote about his travels in the late 13th century. This Noble outfit is based on portraits of him.

MAN OF MYSTERY

SMOOTH SAILING

ORNI BOARD

HELIBOARD!

In 2015 and 2019, Venice's board was the Gondola, which is exactly what it sounds like . . .

In 2016, it was replaced by Orni, a board based on the ornithopter. This was a drawing of an early form of helicopter by the Renaissance artist and inventor Leonardo da Vinci. It remains unknown whether Leonardo ever actually built one!

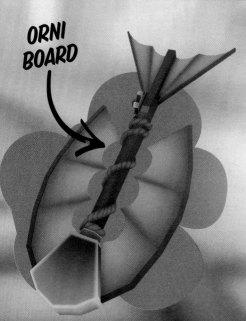

BERLIN

The city with the most graffitied wall in the world!

The German capital is a major graffiti city, boasting some of the most amazing street art you'll see anywhere! It first appeared in *Subway Surfers* in 2018.

After World War II, Germany was split into two countries, and Berlin was divided by a huge wall. But since the city became one again, the Berlin Wall has become one of the most graffitied surfaces in the world! That's a much better use for it . . .

Filled doughnuts were invented in Berlin—in fact, the proper name for one is a "Berliner!"

GRAB THE MIC

Berlin's character, Nina, is a singer. She's named after the punk and new wave singer Nina Hagen. She has very short hair, which is a classic Berlin style . . .

CYBER ATTACK!

SHE'S ELECTRIC!

Her Cyberpunk outfit gives her a green wig and futuristic clothing . . .

And the White Night outfit gives her ace electric-blue hair!

HOVERCHORD

The Rockstar hoverboard is in the shape of a guitar called a Gibson Explorer (used by many musicians, including Matthias Jabs of the German hard rock band the Scorpions) . . .

And the 2021 update added the Buddy Bear board! The Buddy Bears are pieces of Berlin street art and have been exhibited around the world!

ROCKSTAR HOVERBOARD

BUDDY BEAR BOARD

TRANSYLVANIA

This edition is a monster mash-up!

Transylvania is a mountainous part of Romania known for its spectacular scenery. Oh, and vampires—which is why it was introduced as a Halloween edition of *Subway Surfers* in 2015!

There are vampire legends all over the world, but ever since Bram Stoker set his horror novel *Dracula* there in 1897, Transylvania has been associated with vampires like nowhere else. The version of Transylvania in the game is all creepy castles and sinister villages!

The name Dracula comes from the Romanian ruler Vlad Dracula, known as Vlad the Impaler! But the two guys have got nothing to do with each other except the name.

WOLF WEAR

So with this being Transylvania, the land of vampires, obviously the unlockable character is . . . a werewolf! (To be fair, Dracula did also have the power to transform into a big black dog, so not a huge stretch.) Mike wears a Varsity jacket with strong echoes of the 1980s movie *Teen Wolf*.

TEEN WOLF

Or there's the Howl outfit, inspired by the classic video for Michael Jackson's song "Thriller."

And finally the Jager outfit is the kind of thing Transylvanian townsfolk would have worn back in the 19th century!

JAGER OUTFIT

BOOGIE BEAST

PHANTOM

PHANTOM FLIPS

You can also unlock the Zap Sideways upgrade with this board, which allows you to teleport between tracks—reducing the chance of you hitting obstacles.

WHO SAID GOTHS HAVE TO BE MOPEY AND DEPRESSED? SURE, I HANG OUT IN DARK TUNNELS A LOT—BUT I KNOW HOW TO HAVE FUN!

BIG BOW, BIG BOOTS

LUCY

The punk girl of the gang.

Lucy is the easiest character to unlock with coins—just a few sessions should earn enough to buy her for your collection. So, make sure you check the shop if you haven't already bought her!

FULL STEAM AHEAD

The Steam outfit is a look based
on steampunk—a fantasy version
of the Victorian era with weird technology.
Clocks and goggles are standard features
of steampunk outfits. The gold caps
on her boots are a nice touch!

*PUNK BEFORE
PUNK WAS
INVENTED*

Lucy's default outfit
is a white minidress with
a red corset worn over the
top, a bow on her back, and black
boots. There's something very
cyberpunk about her two-tone
hair that's shaved on one side . . .

But our favorite Lucy look is her
Goth outfit! Her red-and-black-
striped leggings are like
something from a Tim
Burton movie.

*GET YOUR
GOTH ON!*

MOSCOW

Rushin' through the Russian capital!

The capital of Russia had to feature in *Subway Surfers*—its metro system is the busiest in Europe, and its stations have some really wild designs! It appeared in September 2013 and September 2019.

When playing this edition, you may have wondered why the subway trains seem to go through palaces, but that's what Moscow metro stations really look like! The metro system isn't just a way of getting around, it's a major tourist attraction, too.

The Bolshoi Theatre in Moscow is the most famous ballet venue in the world and has the biggest ballet company! My parents say that if I keep practicing, maybe I can dance there one day . . .

WHAT FUR?

This isn't the only Russian city to appear in the game—St. Petersburg has been in the Christmas edition in 2017 and 2020, with the character of Nicolai.

NICOLAI

The character for Moscow is Alex, a young Russian dancer who oddly combines a short-sleeved top with furry boots and a cozy hat (this style of hat is called an *ushanka* in Russia).

Alex has one alternative, the Techno outfit, which looks much warmer—and not just because of the flames going up her legs!

HOT STUFF!

ALEX

TED TRICKS

There are two boards for Moscow—Teddy and Leaf.

The bear has often been used as a symbol of Russia in cartoons and has been used by the Russians themselves—the mascot for the 1980 Moscow Olympics was a cute bear called Misha! The Leaf board is autumn-themed.

TEDDY

LEAF

MARRAKESH

What you seek is in the souk!

This Moroccan city is a citadel with fortified walls, dating back about a thousand years. It was first featured in the game back in June 2017.

The real Marrakesh doesn't have a subway, but it does have one of the world's great street racing circuits and hosts several motorsports events every year!

Marrakesh is famous for its traditional street markets, called souks. You can buy almost anything there, from shoes to smartphones! Maybe I'll go down there and see if I can find some new sounds . . .

CHARMING GIRL

Salma was introduced in Marrakesh. She's a snake charmer and street performer who seems to hypnotize a snake with a wind instrument called a *punji*. Check out the snake decoration on her turban!

SNAKE POWER!

In her Nomad outfit, she's got temporary tattoos. Nomads are groups of people who don't make a permanent home in one place—a bit like the surfers, who are always traveling around the globe!

Finally, there's the Talisman outfit, which replaces the snake motif with an impressive jeweled eye!

TERRIFIC TATTOOS

HYPNOTIC GAZE

SLITHER AND SLIDE

The Cobra board might be the most fearsome in the game. You'd get out of the way if you saw that coming, right? However, the cobras found in Morocco are almost always black, not green!

COBRA

HAVE YOU EVER SEEN A SKATER THIS DAPPER?

FRANK

Who *is* that guy?

A creepy presence in the *Subway Surfers'* world, Frank's face is never seen—he always wears a mask. He's certainly not your average skater dude. Look, he doesn't even wear sneakers!

CLOWNING AROUND

A new style for Frank was added in the 2013 New Orleans edition—exactly the same but with a clown mask instead of a rabbit one and a flower instead of a briefcase. Same suit. C'mon, Frank, loosen up a little!

FRANK ALWAYS STICKS WITH HIS SIGNATURE SNAPPY SUIT!

Frank was one of the first characters added to the game in 2012, before the World Tour began. In the animated series, he was seen tracking Jake, but we haven't yet learned why . . .

The original version of Frank wears a rabbit mask and a suit. He always carries a briefcase in his hand—but what's in it? We bet it's empty and he just carries it to look slick.

The Mumbai edition in 2014 added a third style for Frank, with a tiger mask. The briefcase is back, with a tiger tail sticking out of it this time. But the suit is the same. Frank, they do make suits in colors other than black! Guess he must like his shadowy vibe.

CAIRO

Run for your mummy!

The edition featuring the Egyptian capital was the first to take place in Africa! It debuted in September 2014.

The ancient Egyptians are famous for building pyramids as burial sites. Some of the best examples are right on the edge of modern-day Cairo—the Giza Pyramid Complex, along with the Sphinx, which is a vast statue of a mythical creature with the body of a lion and the head of a human!

The Egyptian civilization dates back over five thousand years, and the ancient Egyptians were incredibly advanced technologically. The pyramids are so huge that some people think they couldn't have been made without machinery and must have been built by aliens . . . but I don't think so.

TOP ANKHING

Cairo's character is Jasmine, whose default form sees her dressed like a royal from ancient Egypt (in particular, the legendary queen Cleopatra).

SNAKE BLING

You can unlock the more modern Safari outfit for exploring the Sahara Desert . . .

Or go old-school Egyptian again with the Ankh outfit. The ankh is an Egyptian hieroglyph meaning "life," and the symbol appears in gold on Jasmine's belt.

DESERT CHIC

OLD-SCHOOL EGYPTIAN

CROC & ROLL

Egypt's Nile River has a breed of crocodile named after it, so it's appropriate that the first board for Cairo was the Croc . . .

And in 2018, the Scarab board was added! The scarab was a type of beetle that was a popular design for jewelry in ancient Egypt. It has Smooth Drift and Speed Up upgrades!

CROC

SCARAB

ARABIA

Caught in the Middle East!

Unlike other editions, Arabia is not a city, or even a country—it's a whole region of Asia! It first appeared in the game in April 2015.

Arabia is made up of Bahrain, Iraq, Jordan, Kuwait, Oman, Qatar, Saudi Arabia, and the United Arab Emirates—but Saudi Arabia is the biggest of these countries. It's mostly desert and has no rivers, as you can see from the sandy landscapes of this stage.

A very famous collection of folktales, *The Thousand and One Nights* (often called the *Arabian Nights*), is a big influence on the style of this edition! The story of Aladdin is the best known of these, but it was actually added to the collection later, when it was published in Europe.

PRINCESS POWE

Arabia's character, Amira, is named after the Arabic word for "princess." She certainly likes her jewelry—and she sure knows how to wear it with flair!

TEARDROP TIARA

Her Genie outfit is clearly a big reference to Aladdin, especially the Disney version (genies aren't always blue—that's a Disney thing).

And finally, the Jewel outfit gives her a dress and purple boots.

HAREM PANTS

ROCKET RUG

The board for Arabia, Old Dusty, also comes from *The Thousand and One Nights*—a story where a prince buys a magic carpet that can fly!

It has an upgrade called Dust Trail. In 2017, a second board was added—Jewelled, which is . . . well, covered in jewels.

OLD DUSTY

JEWELLED

HEAVY IS THE HEAD THAT WEARS THE CROWN, THAT'S WHAT THEY ALWAYS SAY. THEY SHOULD TRY WEARING A CROWN MADE OF PAPER! SAVES A LOT OF NECK STRAIN.

#1 IN WHAT, THOUGH?

KING

Who made him king?

He did, apparently! Don't tell anyone, but we think he might have made that crown himself . . .

I'm # 1

King's default outfit features his paper crown and equally homemade royal cape. He wears this over a T-shirt with "I'm #1" on it, which seems to be inspired by the kid on the front of Fatboy Slim's album, *You've Come a Long Way, Baby*.

CASUAL KINGWEAR

Maurice Kingo Erikson isn't actually a member of the *Subway Surfers*— he just hangs around them a lot, whether or not they want him to. He's an only child, homeschooled by his eccentric parents (Jill and Jerry), and he isn't that great at talking to other kids. But he just wants to join in on the fun.

The Count outfit is Halloween-themed, with a tuxedo printed on his T-shirt, and fake fangs. Hope that black hair dye comes out in the shower, King! For the Royal outfit, King has suddenly found himself some regal bling!

MUMBAI

A megacity of movies!

This Indian megacity—one of the largest in the world—first appeared in *Subway Surfers* in January 2014.

Mumbai is a major port city on India's west coast, built on seven islands, with a huge rail network. The long bridges used by the network are a big feature of this edition!

India makes more movies each year than any other country in the world, and the center of Indian cinema is Mumbai! The Hindi-language film industry is nicknamed "Bollywood," a combination of "Hollywood" and the old name for Mumbai, which was Bombay.

ENDLESS RUNNER

Mumbai's character, Jay, is a marathon runner—and he's got a gold medal, so he must be a pretty good one! His default outfit is athletic gear in India's national colors of green, white, and gold.

WIN GOLD

The Blue outfit includes a turban and a sherwani (that's what those long Indian jackets are called).

And the Color Master outfit sees a shirtless Jay covered in paint, a nod to Holi, The Festival of Colors!

COLOR MASTER

BLUE

TIGER FEATS

The first Mumbai hoverboard has tiger stripes in recognition of the Bengal tiger, native to India . . .

And for the re-release in 2018, the Color Cloud board was added. It's not even really a board, it's literally a cloud.

BANGKOK

More bang for your buck!

The capital of Thailand, known for its amazing seafood and colorful nightlife, debuted in the game in November 2014.

Bangkok is one of the fastest-growing cities in the world, going from a population of three million in 1970 to more than ten million today! Its mix of busy streets and tropical beaches feature in the game.

Sadly, Bangkok is one of the cities most under threat from climate change—it often floods, and this will get worse in the future. It's also one of the most polluted because of its busy roads, but better rail networks are helping to fix this!

BEAT BOXER

Bangkok's character is Noon, a *nak muay*. This means she's a practitioner of *Muay Thai*, a popular martial art sometimes called Thai boxing. Her gloves and footwear are important pieces of equipment for a *nak muay*, because you can punch and kick your opponent.

READY FOR ACTION!

Noon's first alternative outfit is the Pink outfit. It's a more relaxed ensemble suitable for a beach party.

And in the Siam outfit, she's dressed for dancing—that spiked hat is a traditional *Chada* dance crown.

PRETTY IN PINK!

SIAM

TURTLE POWER!

Ever wanted to ride a turtle? Well, the Bangkok hoverboard is the next best thing!

Thailand's beaches are top hatching spots for turtles—though unfortunately they're being crowded out by tourists!

BANGKOK HOVERBOARD

THAT LITTLE BROTHER
OF MINE DOESN'T KNOW
REAL MUSIC WHEN
HE HEARS IT . . .

MEET FRESH'S
COOL BIG SIS!

ELLA

Fresher than Fresh!

Fresh's big sister is one of the toughest
characters in the game to unlock—you'll
need to grind your way to a lot of coins
to get her!

ROLLED GOLD

The Gold outfit puts her clothes into another reggae color scheme—black and gold. Jamaica is the birthplace of reggae music, and both colors come from the Jamaican flag—along with green. Originally this outfit came with red shoes, but they were changed to match the rest of the outfit.

REGGAE NINJA!

Ella has a different vibe from Fresh—he's a hip-hop head, but she's all about reggae. In her default outfit, she wears her hair in an Afro and goes for the striped sportswear popular with reggae stars, including Bob Marley . . .

But the Rasta outfit is a beanie hat over dreadlocked hair, and clothes in the classic Rastafarian colors—red, yellow, and green.

STRICTLY ROOTS!

SINGAPORE

The island where East meets West!

Singapore is a city, an island, and a country! It's the second-most densely populated country in the world, and first appeared in the game in June 2016.

Singapore is in southeast Asia, between Malaysia and Indonesia. It's become a very wealthy city in recent years, and its mix of ultra-modern skyscrapers and older buildings can be seen in this edition.

Singapore used to be part of the British Empire, and English is still one of the main languages there, along with Mandarin. It's one of the most multicultural countries in the world!

TIGER QU**EEN**

Singapore offers you Jia, a fierce street skater with a reversed baseball cap and a black cat on her T-shirt.

RAWR!

The tiger is one of Singapore's national symbols, so Jia's first alternative is the Wild outfit . . .

The unicorn isn't one of Singapore's national symbols, but Jia's Unicorn outfit is still ace! Her hoodie has ears and a horn on the hood, and rainbow stripes on the sleeves.

EARNING YOUR STRIPES!

LION

LION BLING

The lion is another of Singapore's national symbols, hence the design of this board! In the 2019 update, a 1980s surfboard-style board called Retro Wave was introduced along with a character named Maeko—both came from the Chinese version of the game.

BEIJING

No tagging the Great Wall of China!

The capital of China has the longest and busiest subway system on Earth, so it's no surprise to see it here—it was introduced as a World Tour stage in August 2013.

Beijing is one of the world's oldest cities, and today it's one of the biggest! Because it's been an important city for so long, it's got amazing palaces and temples, and the Great Wall of China runs through it—as featured in the game.

In the middle of Beijing, there's a huge palace named the Forbidden City and it has 9,999 rooms! See, you call something the Forbidden City and I immediately want to go there! But actually, it's not that forbidden—it gets 19 million visitors a year!

SUN KING

MONKEY MAGIC

Beijing's character, Sun, is named after Sun Wukong, the Monkey King of the 16th-century Chinese tale *Journey to the West*—a story that's been performed over and over again. Sun's default outfit is based on how the Monkey King is traditionally pictured, including his makeup.

The Spot outfit sees him dressed as a Buddhist monk, like the main character of *Journey to the West*, Xuanzang.

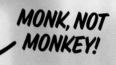

MONK, NOT MONKEY!

BAMBOO BANGER!

China is the natural habitat of the panda, which is celebrated on Beijing's board.

In 2020, another board, Aero, was brought from the Chinese version into the global version, along with Monkbot, a Chinese robot.

PANDA

AERO

I WILL STRIKE WHEN YOU LEAST EXPECT IT. NOT NOW. OR NOW. LOOK, IT WON'T BE WHEN YOU'RE WATCHING ME.

THE COLOR OF NIGHT!

NINJA

The moonlight shadow!

We don't know his name! He's known only as Ninja, and he always hides his face. Ninjas operated as spies and assassins in Japan, mostly around the 15th and 16th centuries. They specialized

He's on fire!

The default outfit for Ninja is black (or maybe it's very, very dark gray?) with a red belt. Check out his wooden sandals, too! They don't look super stealthy, but who knows . . . The Flame outfit is not how ninjas generally used to look.

FLAME OUTFIT

in unseen movement and surprise attack . . . which is why the classic ninja uniform is black, so they could move about, unseen in the darkness.

Obviously these are good skills if you're a subway surfer—you can get in there, tag a wall, and get out before anyone even sees you!

Plus, Japanese words make GREAT tags.

The Yang outfit is named after the Chinese concept of yin and yang. This is the idea that things that seem like opposites can exist in balance—which is why this outfit is the opposite color from his normal one. Not so good for moving through shadows, but guess it might be useful if you need to sneak around in the snow?

TOKYO

The megacity to end all megacities!

The Japanese capital is the world's biggest city, and has two subway systems! Tokyo first appeared in *Subway Surfers* in May 2013.

Lots of things give Japanese cities their distinctive look, and you can see many of them in the game—the red *torii* gates, seen at Shinto shrines, run across the tracks, and there are vending machines lining the sides. You may be able to spot the world's tallest tower, the Tokyo Skytree, on the skyline!

Tokyo is one of the coolest places in the world, and the coolest place in Tokyo is Akihabara! It's the electronics district, and it's full of shops selling computer games and manga! I could stay there forever—maybe one day I will . . .

SCHOOLED

UNIFORM LOOK

Tokyo's character is Harumi—you can tell she's a teenager because her default outfit is a Japanese school uniform.

But when she's out of school, Harumi likes to dress up! Her Meow outfit consists of a black dress, electric-blue wig, kitty ears, and whiskers painted on her face . . .

The Fury outfit gives her a superhero vibe—or maybe a supervillain? She has a black mask and a white wig.

CAT-NESS EVER-KEEN

FURY!

LUCKY BLOSSOM

The Kitty hoverboard depicts a traditional Japanese symbol of luck, the Beckoning Cat.

And there's also the Cherry board, which celebrates Japan's famous flowering cherry trees!

KITTY HOVERBOARD

CHERRY BOARD

SEOUL

Giving a new meaning to Seoul music!

The K-pop capital has become one of the world's most exciting cities in recent years! It came to *Subway Surfers* in February 2014.

There's a good chance the device you play *Subway Surfers* on was designed in Seoul—Samsung and LG are both based there. The city has numerous graffiti spots, the most famous of which is the Sinchon graffiti tunnel in the west of the city. The Mullae Art Village also has spectacular painted rooftops.

Most singers go through years of training to prepare for life as a K-pop star, including the awesome dance routines they perform onstage. The cost of this has been estimated at $3 million per trainee! And I thought I was under a lot of pressure at ballet school . . .

SEOUL SINGER

Mina, the unlockable character for Seoul, is a South Korean girl. Her default outfit is casual wear.

ROBOT DANCE!

The Robo outfit has joints and boots that give her a robotic look, reflecting South Korea's cutting-edge robotics industry!

The Pop look gives her a popstar-style uniform that's sort of military, except for the fact that it's pink!

In 2019, a second character was introduced, named Rin—the first character from the Chinese edition of the game to be brought into the global version!

K-POP STYLE

MEET RIN

STICK OF GUM

BUBBLEGUM

POP!

The Seoul hoverboard is the Bubblegum board with POP written across it—very appropriate for the home of K-pop. Bubblegum is a subgenre of particularly cute and sweet K-pop, with sugary treats often featured in the videos—examples include "Jelly" by Jeon Soyeon and "Just Right" by Got7.

MY DATABANKS CONTAIN OVER THREE MILLION TAGS IN TWO HUNDRED LANGUAGES! I CAN ALSO SPELL-CHECK YOUR TAGS, IF YOU LIKE.

MAGNETIC PERSONALITY

TAGBOT

The cyber-surfer!

This metal dude is another easy character to unlock with coins. But Tagbot isn't the only robot character in the game! The golden Boombot can be unlocked with any purchase from the store, and the 2021 Space Station edition featured Spacebot and Frankette (a cross between Rabbot and Frank, weirdly).

BLEEP BLOOP

The Space outfit has several touches based on R2-D2 from *Star Wars*—the two little attachments on his head, the design on his chest, and his overall blue-and-white color scheme . . .

IS THIS THE DROID YOU'RE LOOKING FOR?

There are others, too! Judging by his hat, the default look for Tagbot is inspired by Jake. But can Jake remove his head to use as a basketball? Not that we know of!

The Toy outfit gives Tagbot another new color scheme, as well as a key in his head for winding him up. Old-fashioned? Maybe! But it's also very eco-friendly! We just hope he doesn't wind down in the middle of a run—that'd be annoying if he suddenly needed winding up again when the guard and his dog were catching up . . .

BALI

Time to hit the beach!

Bali is an area of Indonesia with glorious beaches, which make it a hugely popular tourist spot! This edition came out in July 2019.

The spectacular coast and marine life, which is such a big feature of Bali, is also big in the game—it takes you through magical and secluded coves.

Pink freight trucks and rainbow arches make this one of the most colorful editions of the game—but there's also a distinct eco theme . . .

Bali is in the Coral Triangle, a major spot for coral reefs. Coral reefs around the world are under threat from pollution, so there's a big conservation effort right now to make sure they are still there for future generations!

MEI DAY

Bali's character is Mei, a surfer girl—the south coast of Bali is one of the world's great surfing spots. Her sun hat looks big enough to cover the whole gang!

EPIC SHADE

The Islander outfit sees Mei dressed up ready for festival time.

In the Indonesian language, "bumi" means "earth," so Mei's Bumi outfit is green and decorated with flowers.

DOWN TO EARTH!

SNAKE SKIN

The Naga is a mythical serpent, similar in appearance to a Chinese dragon without legs. The first hoverboard for Bali pays tribute to this magical creature.

When Bali reappeared in 2020, it was with a new board, Coral, reflecting Bali's precious coral reefs.

CORAL

MYTHICAL SERPENT

SYDNEY

Get down under!

This isn't the capital of Australia, but it is the biggest city—and by far the most recognizable. The Sydney edition debuted in April 2013.

Sydney has a huge natural harbor, which is the location of Australia's most famous building, the Sydney Opera House, and the Sydney Harbour Bridge. The game includes the country's distinctive red-rock landscape, as well as signs to warn of kangaroos crossing!

The Ku-ring-gai Chase National Park in Sydney contains over 1,500 pieces of Aboriginal rock art made by the indigenous peoples of the land. Some of those pieces are 5,000 years old. They were the original taggers!

MOI, AUSSIE

DIVING FOR PEARLS

Surfer girl Kim is the character for Sydney. Her default outfit is all set for the beach—check out her seashell necklace . . .

The Dive outfit gives her a wet suit and snorkel!

And the Coast outfit has a cowgirl hat and boots. (Yes, they have cowboys and cowgirls in Australia, too.)

NEW WAVE STYLE

RAY BOARD

GET BACK

OUTBACK

Every time Sydney appears in the game, it has a new board. The original edition featured the Outback board, with a design based on Aboriginal art.

In 2015, it was Wave Rider, which resembles a surfboard . . .

2016 brought us Ray, which is designed like a manta ray fish.

WAVE RIDER

GIVE ME AN "S"! GIVE ME A "U"! GIVE ME A "B"! GIVE ME A "W"! GIVE ME AN "A"! GIVE ME A "Y"... WHAT D'YOU MEAN, WHY? IT'S TODAY'S WORD HUNT WORD! LOOK, I JUST NEED THE "Y" AND I'VE COMPLETED IT!!

FITNESS FANATIC

TASHA

Bringing good cheer!

Tasha is another coin-unlockable character—a blond cheerleader. You wouldn't think she's the sort of person you'd find tagging subway tunnels, would you?

GO, TEAM!

Her Cheer outfit sees Tasha go full cheerleader, with a purple uniform and pom-poms, and her hair tied up in pigtails.

SHAKING HER POM-POM

You shouldn't judge by appearances—and Tasha certainly has the fitness and acrobatic skills you need to avoid getting caught!

Tasha's default clothing is a training outfit, with a white tank top and her hair tied back in a headband—in fact, it's quite similar to Tricky's . . .

The Gym outfit has Tasha dressed for a workout, with leg warmers and a high ponytail—again, quite similar to Tricky's . . . but who wore it better? You decide! The color scheme is very early 1990s—in fact, we're pretty sure there was a level of the original *Sonic the Hedgehog* that was in those colors!

SURF QUIZ

Test your *Subway Surfers* knowledge!

1. In which country was *Subway Surfers* invented?

2. Which character is a zombie—and which has a zombie variant?

3. What's Tricky's real name?

4. What's Fresh's favorite sport?

5. What animal does Bjarki carry?

6. How many UFOs are needed to unlock Yutani?

7. Which explorer is Venice's character named after?

8. What alien technology did Yutani use to invent the hoverboard?

9. What type of monster is the unlockable character for Transylvania?

10. How many robot rabbits have been featured as characters?

11. What are Lucy's alternative outfits called?

12. What are Frank's three masks?

13 What does Amira's name mean in Arabic?

1 What does it say on King's T-shirt?

15 Who was the first character from the Chinese version of the game to be introduced into the main game?

16 And which edition were they introduced in?

17 Which two editions have featured the Pixel Heart hoverboard?

18 Which edition changed from daytime to nighttime?

19 Which city was the first World Tour edition?

20 Which character has more different outfits than any other?

HAWAII

A Pacific paradise!

Hawaii is the most far-flung state of the USA—it's in the middle of the Pacific Ocean! It entered *Subway Surfers* in February 2015.

The Hawaiian archipelago is made up of 137 volcanic islands, including some of the most active volcanoes in the world!

Watch out for lava on the tracks (not really—at least, we've never seen any in the game!).

Hawaiians have a traditional type of party called a *lu'au*, which is held outdoors and often involves ukulele music and hula dancing. This began in 1819 when King Kamehameha II broke with the old custom where men and women ate separately. Foods served at a *lu'au* include *kālua pua'a* (roast pig) and squid *lu'au*!

ALOHA!

Izzy, Hawaii's unlockable character, has a default outfit made of leaves and grass, and wears body and face paint—all traditional aspects of Hawaiian culture.

THE LEAF LOOK

But the Aloha outfit (named for the Hawaiian word for "hello") gives him a modern beach look, with a pink lei.

"Laki maika'i" means "good luck" in Hawaiian, so Izzy's Tiki mask in his default outfit means that he is wishing you good luck!

PARTY TIME

TRICKY TIKI

UKULELE

Like many Pacific island cultures, Hawaii has a tradition of making carvings representing the first man, whose name was Tiki. The Tiki hoverboard honors this with a face in the Tiki style!

The 2017 re-release of Hawaii brought a new board, Ukulele. It was shaped like the simple guitar-like instrument.

TIKI HOVERBOARD

SAN FRANCISCO

Turn on, tune in, surf away!

San Francisco—possibly the trendiest city in America—is in California, on the west coast of the country. This edition first appeared in January 2016.

The most famous part of the San Francisco skyline is the huge Golden Gate Bridge—which is perfect for *Subway Surfers*! So of course, the train tracks have to run across it! Unfortunately in real life, it's just a road bridge. Boring! We also love the retro gaming graffiti on this edition . . .

San Francisco became the center of hippie culture in the 1960s, and it's still got a lot of that vibe today. But it's also right next to Silicon Valley, so the tech industry is a big part of San Francisco, too.

FLOWER CHILD

Jenny, the unlockable character for San Francisco, is a Chinese American hippie girl. Her default outfit gives her a headband and big 1960s glasses.

GROOVY GIRL

Her Party outfit calls back to her Chinese heritage—it's a *cheongsam* (slim-fitting Chinese dress), and the design fits with her hippie look . . .

The Pixel outfit shows Jenny is a retro gaming fan, with pixelated glasses and T-shirt design, and a handheld console on her belt.

KEEPING IT REAL

PIXEL

PEACE OUT!

The Groovy hoverboard bears the peace symbol against a psychedelic backdrop. Far-out, man! And to go with Jenny's Pixel outfit, there's the Pixel Heart board. It was added in the 2019 re-release, for those who really love retro gaming!

GROOVY HOVERBOARD

MUST...TAG...
WALLS...

GONE GREEN

ZOE

Playing dead.

Zoe doesn't talk too much, but you'll be
surprised how fast she can move when
she's being chased! She's also one of
the hardest characters to unlock . . .

READY TO ORDER?

Zoe's default outfit suggests that she was just an ordinary country girl, before she got bitten . . .

But there are more clues in her Curly outfit! Here she's got very different hair and cat-eye glasses, giving her a 1950s look. So either she has a retro style, or she's just been dead since the 1950s. Plus, she wears a name tag suggesting that she was a waitress . . .

DEAD COOL!

Zoe is a zombie. (In fact, is Zoe short for Zombie? Who knows? Zoe probably doesn't.) But she's a pretty friendly zombie, and hasn't tried to eat any of the gang's brains . . . yet. You might think of zombies as being slow, but don't be deceived—Zoe can be fast as any of the gang when Guard is on her tail!

The Biker outfit kits Zoe out in a motorcycle helmet and leathers. We're glad she's sensible enough to wear a helmet when she rides a motorbike because if she had an accident she might . . . well, she's not going to die, but her head might come off, which would make eating tricky, wouldn't it?

SEATTLE

Home of computers and coffee!

This coastal American city is so far north it's almost in Canada! Seattle was introduced into the game in November 2020.

Seattle was originally based around the logging industry, but today it's one of the greenest cities—both in terms of the number of trees it has and its eco-friendliness. Its most recognizable landmark is the Space Needle, which you'll see in the background of this edition!

These days, Seattle is best known for being a technology center—Amazon was founded here. Microsoft's founder Bill Gates was born here and the company is based in nearby Redmond, along with Nintendo's American headquarters! Oh, and Starbucks is from here, too.

GAME BOY

Seattle's character is Andy, who combines the tech side of Seattle with his retro gaming T-shirt, and its logging history with his lumberjack shirt (a popular piece of clothing in Seattle's grunge rock scene of the 1990s).

Andy's alternative outfit, the Gamer outfit, mixes retro and cutting-edge gaming technology. He's got VR goggles, and wears a glove that looks like the Power Glove, a peripheral for the old Nintendo Entertainment System!

PERIPHERAL VISION

HIGH SCORER

PIXEL HEART

HEART TRANSPLANT

For the first time ever, a *Subway Surfers* edition had no new board—instead the Pixel Heart board was reintroduced. Well, it fit in nicely!

Maybe Seattle will come back with a board of its own sometime? Watch this space . . .

VANCOUVER

Canada's city of glass and greenery!

This futuristic Canadian city on the coast is supposedly one of the best places in the world to live! This stage first appeared in May 2014.

If some of the trains on this edition look a little different, that's because they're actually trams! Vancouver doesn't have a subway, but it has a big tram network! The city also has dense woodland nearby, which features in the game.

You've probably seen parts of Vancouver without realizing it. Lots of films and TV shows set in the USA or elsewhere in the world are actually made in Vancouver because of its great production facilities. Films made there include *Diary of a Wimpy Kid*, *Deadpool*, *Sonic the Hedgehog*, and *Doctor Strange in the Multiverse of Madness*.

⬛ COOL

SCOUT'S HONOR

Olivia, the Vancouver character, is a Girl Scout who wears a furry hat with a bear's paw print on the front. Do they give out merit badges for graffiti? If so, Olivia's probably earned hers already!

The Skate outfit isn't about skateboarding— it's about ice hockey! This is Canada's national sport, and Olivia's wearing her country's team colors here (though they're not the colors of Vancouver's NHL team, the Canucks).

READY FOR THE RINK

ANTLER ANTICS

You could also use the Moose board to scare an irritating brother or sister, because it's quite alarming. This board popped up again as a season hunt reward in Seattle!

MOOSE

LITTLE ROCK

Lost in the supermarket!

Little what? The state capital of Arkansas isn't exactly little. It's a city, but it's one of the smallest cities featured in the game! It was introduced in July 2020.

The name Little Rock comes from a rock formation on the Arkansas River, which was easy to recognize and became an important landmark for travelers! If you're wondering whether there was also a Big Rock—yeah, that's what they named the quarry on the other side of the river.

This edition was a first for *Subway Surfers* because it was a tie-in with the Walmart chain of supermarkets. That's why it's set in Little Rock—the Walmart chain began in Arkansas in 1945. Parts of this edition involve the player running through a Walmart store!

CHECK IT OUT

Jack, the character for Little Rock, wears a button-up shirt and red tie—dressed for work! He's got a Walmart hat, so it seems like he must work there. No tagging while you're on the job, Jack!

HAPPY TO HELP!

Jack's other outfit, the Dapper outfit, gives him a yellow plaid jacket and matching shoes, but he keeps his baseball cap on—all of which gives him a 1950s vibe.

LITTLE ROCK 'N' ROLL!

CRUISING!

The hoverboard, Betty, is an old-fashioned pickup truck with no wheels. The license plate says BETTY, but the back bumper says WALTON, referring to Walmart's founder, Sam Walton. It was the eighth car-themed board in the game!

BETTY

I SURF ANYWHERE... BEACHES, SUBWAYS... IT'S ALL JUST BOARDS TO ME!

WET SUIT AND TRUNKS

BRODY

Too cool for school . . .

Brody's a young lifeguard who spends his days on the beach, keeping you safe and watching out for sharks . . . while working on his tan. Not the kind of guy you'd expect to find running through tunnels!

DIFFERENT CLASS

Brody's first alternative is the Posh outfit—a classy polo shirt, just the thing for hanging out on a millionaire's yacht. Is Brody posh, though? Maybe that's why he costs so much to unlock . . .

TAILORED
SHORTS

Brody is one of the most expensive characters in the game to unlock. You might have to double up by watching an ad or two if you want to get him . . .

He's named after one of the characters who hunts the shark in the film *Jaws*.

The Chill outfit offers a more hippieish look, with round colored sunglasses and a massive peace sign hung around his neck. Brody doesn't look like he needs a special outfit to get any more chill! He looks like he'd get on pretty well with Jenny in this outfit, though—maybe we'll see him heading to San Francisco . . .

CHICAGO

Breeze into the Windy City!

This American city is famous for great music and great junk food! It first appeared in the January 2018 edition of the game.

Chicago stands on the shore of the huge Lake Michigan, and has a long pier named Navy Pier, which was used by the military and for shipping. But nowadays it's one big tourist attraction, with a funfair, restaurants, and shops! That's where the huge ferris wheel you can see in the background of this edition comes from.

Chicago is the home of the deep-dish pizza, which has a thick crust and lots of filling—with the cheese on the bottom and the tomato on top! Even I can't eat more than one of these in one sitting—and believe me, I've tried!

IN TOUCH

The character for Chicago is E.Z., who wears a baseball cap with a *C* for Chicago on it.

EASY FIT

You can also get him in the Touchdown outfit, an American football uniform . . .

And finally, the Jive outfit casts him as a jazz musician complete with trombone. All set for a jam session with the hepcats of the jazz scene, daddio!

JAZZ

HOT DOG

TAKE NOTE

The 2020 release of Chicago came with a new hoverboard, Jazz, celebrating the city's amazing musical innovators—with options to add a horn (speed up) or saxophones (super jump)! And because jazz clubs come alive at night, for the first time, an edition was changed from daytime to nighttime.

Another great Chicago street food is the Chicago-style hot dog, made of beef and topped with pickles and mustard. (Don't put ketchup on it, Chicagoans will disown you!) So that's why Hotdog is the board for this edition.

I MUCH PREFER BEING ON THE WORLD TOUR ... AT HOME, EVERYONE RECOGNIZES ME! HOW AM I SUPPOSED TO HAVE ANY FUN??

COOL IN THE HEAT

PRINCE K

Actual *Subway Surfers* royalty!

Prince K is the hardest character in the game to unlock with coins! Unlike King, where it's just a nickname, Prince K is an actual member of a royal family from the Middle East—so his family wouldn't be too happy if they learned he was hopping around the world tagging subways!

PRINCE CHARMING

All Prince K's outfits come with a hood, called a *kaffiyeh*, and sunglasses—the first is more sporty, though check out that gold watch and matching sneakers!

The Jag outfit has a leopard-skin pattern and adds matching gold shades . . .

COOL CAT

It's a good thing the Surfers have some wealthy members though—traveling around the world isn't cheap, even if there are plenty of coins to be found on the train tracks. Without Prince K, the World Tour would be more of a Local Towns Tour!

The Shine outfit adds some extra bling! That all-white clothing would be very easy to get dirty down on the subway tracks, though. And we're not sure why he's got one long trouser leg and one short one. Maybe it's a fashion thing that we haven't heard of yet? Probably next year everyone will be cutting off one trouser leg.

NEW YORK

The inspiration for *Subway Surfers*!

The Big Apple is the home of graffiti, so it's appropriate that it was the first ever World Tour edition of *Subway Surfers* back in January 2013!

New York is the name of the state, but also its largest metropolis. The city's subway is the biggest in the world, with 472 stations! The yellow cab is another recognizable symbol of New York City. Look for them on the streets when you're high up! And if you reach the upper levels, you may find yourself in Central Park.

Graffiti as a form of art began in Philadelphia in the 1960s, but it made a big impact on New York City in the 1970s as part of the growing hip-hop scene. Taggers put their tags on subway cars, so their work was seen all over the city! Some hated the graffiti and wanted it removed, but some loved the underground art scene!

GET TO NY

Tony, this edition's unlockable character, has true New York street style—puffer vest and work boots . . .

We don't know why his first alternative is named the Folk outfit, but it adds a hat!

And the Game outfit sees him dressed to go to a baseball game—but is he a Yankees fan or a Mets fan? The Mets' uniform is lighter blue so we'll go with that.

HATMAN RETURNS

SHADY CHARACTER

GO, SPORTS, GO!

TAKING LIBERTY

New York City's most famous landmark, the Statue of Liberty, is depicted on the original hoverboard for this edition.

The 2018 edition added the Yellow Cab board . . .

And the Uprock board, with its spray can design, appeared in 2021!

WANT A RIDE?

UPROCK

LIBERTY

CAMBRIDGE

Welcome to spooky town!

Not the English city—this is Cambridge, Massachusetts, on the east coast of America! It was the Halloween edition in 2020.

Massachusetts's dark past is connected to the witch trials that happened in Salem in the late 17th century. Ever since then, movies, TV shows, and books about witches have been set in the area. *Sabrina the Teenage Witch* even has a cat named Salem!

Cambridge was named after the English city, which has one of the world's most famous universities. Today it has a famous university of its own—Harvard, the oldest university in the USA and often ranked as the best in the world! And there aren't any monsters there really . . . I think . . .

MEET THE SCREAM TEAM

For the first time, an edition introduced three characters at once! The Scream Team are a bunch of monstrous high school students . . .

Cathy's octopus-like face is inspired by the legendary monster Cthulhu.

Morgan likes to read—well, she's got plenty of eyes to do it with. She's based on the shoggoths, which also appear in the Cthulhu stories, but she's cuter than they are.

Swamp monster Noel is equipped with a charming old-fashioned swimsuit and goggles (though you'd think he wouldn't need them, what with being a swamp monster).

MORGAN   CATHY

NOEL

BEELZE-BOARD!

BEELZEBOOK

The board is Beelzebook, a witch's spellbook—although that bookmark looks a little like a tongue . . .

And Beelzebook is a play on the name Beelzebub, the prince of the devils from the Bible.

> *ROAR!*
> *WHAT ELSE DO YOU*
> *EXPECT ME TO SAY?*
> *I'M A DINOSAUR.*

DINO

Dino can be unlocked simply by connecting your account with Facebook. Dino is blue, like the Facebook logo—but the zip down the front is a telltale clue. This is someone in a dinosaur costume—but who? Maybe it's secretly Yutani again . . .

BOOMBOT

I DON'T BREAK DOWN WHEN I BREAK-DANCE!

Boombot is a gold robot with the ability to remove its floating boom-box head and break-dance. Useful! You can obtain it by making any purchase in the store.

BOOM BOX!

PEOPLE THINK I'M MYSTERIOUS BECAUSE I WEAR THIS RESPIRATOR MASK... REALLY, I JUST WANT TO AVOID BREATHING IN PAINT FUMES. IT'S GOOD SENSE!

READY FOR ACTION!

MISS MAIA

Miss Maia first appeared in the 2019 edition of San Francisco, unlockable with a promo code. You can't get her with the code anymore, but she can still be bought with keys!

NEW ORLEANS

Deep in the Deep South!

This hot and sticky city in the state of Louisiana has a reputation for being America's most haunted—hence it was selected to be the second Halloween edition of the World Tour in 2013! In fact, this was the first Halloween edition to have a specific location.

New Orleans is also known for its food, music, and parties! The Mardi Gras carnival takes place every year, and goes on for two weeks, with at least one parade every day leading up to Fat Tuesday.

New Orleans is strongly associated with Voodoo, a religion developed by African people who'd been enslaved and brought to Louisiana. One Voodoo belief is that making and wearing charms can heal or protect you—or harm others! I guess our version of that is the hoverboard . . .

▮▮ VOODOO

The New Orleans character, Eddy, is dressed as a Voodoo priest, with a skeleton pattern on his chest, skull makeup on his face, and a top hat with a skull on it (we're noticing a pattern here) . . .

The Trick outfit, released in 2014, casts him as a stage magician wearing a tuxedo with playing cards in his hat.

TRICK OR TREAT?

SMART BONES

CARVE IT UP!

With its jack-o'-lantern grin, the Pumpkin hoverboard offers classic Halloween stylings.

The 2018 edition brought back all the characters and boards from previous Halloween editions, so always check the game around special occasions— it can be a great time to fill gaps in your collection!

PUMPKIN HOVERBOARD

HAVANA

The city of dance!

The capital of Cuba, known as the center of dance, was the first Caribbean stop for the World Tour in September 2016!

Havana is divided into three areas—the old town, which still has the walls built to protect it during the Spanish-American War of 1898; Vedado, the business district; and finally the more modern suburbs. The game is based around Old Havana—the colorful buildings in this stage are common in Caribbean countries.

Havana has an impressive ballet school and a successful international ballet festival—and Cuba is also the birthplace of mambo music, which helped give rise to salsa, one of the most popular forms of dance in the world!

RAMONA CAN FIX IT!

Havana's character, Ramona, is a mechanic in her original outfit, which could be useful when your hoverboard breaks down . . .

Her Pina outfit is a more relaxed ensemble, with flowers in her hair . . .

And the Elegant outfit sees her dressed for dancing!

RAMONA

LET'S DANCE!

1950S CLASSIC

The Chrome board is styled like a 1950s car, such as a Cadillac—perfect for cruising!

CRUISE THE STREETS IN CHROME STYLE!

MEXICO

Take a return trip to Mexico City!

The Day of the Dead is Mexico's most important festival, and *Subway Surfers* used it as the theme for Halloween in 2018!

An earlier edition in 2014 took place in Mexico's capital, Mexico City, with the unlockable character of Rosa and a cactus board, Prickly. The Mexico edition has a different name and new unlockables, but the actual setting for this level is still based on Mexico City.

Mexican people celebrate *Día de los Muertos*, the Day of the Dead, every November 1. Families gather to remember the dead and leave offerings to them to encourage their souls to visit. It's about celebrating loved ones' lives rather than being sad that they're gone!

MEET MANNY

Mexico's character is Manny, a skeleton kid wearing typical skater clothing . . .

READY TO SKATE!

But the Mariachi outfit casts him as a member of a mariachi band, a traditional Mexican musical style involving guitars, violins, and trumpets. His vibrant suit, hat, and makeup are all very Day of the Dead!

The Luchador outfit is the style worn by Mexican wrestlers! Although, seeing as Manny has zero muscles, he's probably not the most fearsome opponent in the ring . . .

DEAD COOL

The Casket board is designed like a coffin, which might come in handy if you have a really bad crash!

THE CASKET

PRICKLY

117

THIS JOB WOULD BE GREAT IF IT WEREN'T FOR THOSE KIDS. I'D NEVER HAVE TO DO ANYTHING! ALTHOUGH THEN THE BOSS MIGHT FIRE ME FOR DOING NOTHING . . .
TED LUTZ
DOG

GUA D A D DOG

Don't let them catch you!

This long-suffering guardian of the subways is forever chasing after the Surfers. "Guard" and his dog are the only non-playable characters in the game!

Subway guard Ted Lutz certainly gets around—wherever the Surfers are in the world, he's always the one trying to grab them for tagging the walls! He's not as fast as the kids, but he knows these subways inside out and doesn't crash into anything— so he's never far behind.

Guard's loyal dog is usually a bull terrier . . . but this sometimes changes in different editions.

DRESSED FOR THE OCCASION

Guard has more different outfits than any other character, because new editions bring new outfits!

At Halloween, he's always dressed as Frankenstein's monster (and has a skeleton dog) . . .

In Christmas editions, he's Santa Claus and his dog is Rudolph the Red-Nosed Reindeer . . .

At Easter, he has on an Easter Bunny suit! Does he enjoy wearing these costumes, or does the subway company make him do it . . . ?

In certain stages, he's dressed as a local law enforcement official— a Mountie in Vancouver, an NYPD officer in New York . . .

PERU

Time to explore an ancient civilization!

Peru is a megadiverse South American country that includes desert plains, mountains, and tropical rain forests. It also has an incredible history! It first appeared in the game in May 2016.

Peru was once the center of the Incan Empire, which ruled most of the west coast of South America by the time it was conquered by the Spanish in the 16th century. This edition mostly focuses on the Incas rather than modern-day Peru—parts of it are based on Machu Picchu, the mountainous Incan citadel that lay abandoned for centuries and fell into ruin.

Peru has one of the oldest civilizations in the world! But not in the universe. There are much older civilizations out there, trust me . . .

CLIMB WITH CARLOS

Mountaineer Carlos is your unlockable character for Peru, equipped to tackle the Andes—the longest mountain range in the world!

The Inca outfit harks back to the past—his robes and headdress resemble Incan ceremonial wear.

In the 2017 update, the Poncho outfit was added. It can get cold on those mountaintops, so we're glad to see he has a hat.

ANCIENT HISTORY

MAYAN DESIGN

The Peru board draws its design from farther north in Mesoamerica. It's inspired by Mayan calendars, which are round like a clock. It can be equipped with the Zap Sideways upgrade!

The 2020 edition brought a board from the Chinese edition—Goat!

RIO DE JANEIRO

Join the party!

Rio de Janeiro, the home of the world's biggest carnival, is no longer Brazil's official capital—but it's still the party capital! It first appeared in the game in January 2013.

Each year, Brazilians mark the beginning of Lent with a carnival on the Friday before Mardi Gras. These events have become massive, and the biggest one happens in Rio, with over two million people attending! You may also spot the famous mountaintop statue, Christ the Redeemer, in the background of this edition.

Brazil is a soccer-crazy country, and when Rio hosted the World Cup in 1950, the final match had almost 200,000 fans present—the greatest number to ever attend a soccer match!

SAMBA TIME!

Carmen, the Rio character, is named after the famous samba singer and dancer Carmen Miranda. She has two carnival-style outfits—the default one uses the colors of the Brazilian flag, blue, green, white, and yellow . . .

BRAZILIAN COLORS

And the Shake outfit is in pink and purple.

The Team outfit is totally different, giving Carmen a jacket and skirt in Brazilian colors—which are also the colors of the national soccer team! It fits with the overall sports theme of the 2016 edition.

SHAKE IT!

RIO BOARDS

Rio has had a new board in every update so far! First, there was the Toucan board, designed like the tropical bird.

Then in 2015, the Birdie board, designed like a rainbow-colored feather, appeared.

In 2016, Rio hosted the Olympic Games, and to mark the event, this edition returned again with a special Medal board.

At the end of 2018, Rio was brought back for New Year, and the Rocket board was available!

BIRDIE

ROCKET

TOUCAN

BUENOS AIRES

Time to tango.

The capital of Argentina is one of the most multicultural cities in the Americas—people there have roots from all over the world! It first came to *Subway Surfers* in April 2018.

Pedro de Mendoza named the city "Ciudad de la Santísima Trinidad y Puerto de Santa María del Buen Aire," which is Spanish for "City of the Most Holy Trinity and Port of Saint Mary of the Fair Winds." It's not surprising that it got shortened to Buenos Aires.

All the different influences on Buenos Aires mean its architecture is really varied, as you can see in the game—parts of it are European-looking, parts are more typically Latin American. Its most famous landmark is the Obelisco—that white needle thing—which was built in 1936 to mark four hundred years since the city was founded!

STREET-SMART GAUCHO

Sofia, the Buenos Aires character, has some of the most varied outfits of any character in the game! Her default is a street-smart look with headphones and a baseball cap . . .

But the Gaucho outfit is totally different! Gauchos were the South American version of cowboys—skilled, brave horse riders, some of whom became legends. Sofia's look here is typical of gauchos.

And the Tango outfit sees Sofia ready to engage in Argentina's national dance!

MAKE A SPLASH!

The Splash hoverboard looks like a colorful jet plane with turbines on its wings and tail!

The 2020 edition added the Roto board, with a drone design.

THE SPLASH

SPACE STATION

Skate through space!

This January 2021 edition put *Subway Surfers* in space for the first time! What's next? Mars, probably . . .

This was not the first edition to deal with space travel. The 2019 Houston edition was set around a NASA launch facility—but it's the first to go into space! It's not actually part of the World Tour because, well, it's not in the world. The trapped aliens you see are actually from another game made by SYBO, *Blades of Brim*.

The International Space Station, or ISS, was launched in 1998 and has circled the Earth ever since! It's jointly operated by the space agencies of Russia, Europe, Japan, Canada, and the USA. It looks a little different from this edition— you can't go running around it!

SPACE BUDDIES

SPACE BEATS

Two limited characters were introduced—Spacebot has the same design as Boombot, but with a different color scheme and the Roto board's logo on his head.

Frankette is much creepier—similar in shape to Rabbot, but with a mask and decoration to make her look like Frank? We're not sure we want to unlock her!

FRANKETTE

SECRET SOCIETY

FUTURISTIC BOARDS

Three futuristic boards were unlockable in Space Station—the same design in three different colors. First, Secret Society . . .

Then Discovery, named after a NASA shuttle that ran missions to the ISS and put the Hubble Space Telescope into orbit . . .

And finally Endeavor, named after a space shuttle, too—the command module of the Apollo 15 spacecraft was also called Endeavor.

ANSWERS

SURF QUIZ ANSWERS

1) DENMARK
2) ZOE AND JAKE
3) BEATRICE FAIRCHILD
4) BASKETBALL
5) A SHEEP
6) 500
7) MARCO POLO
8) ALIEN, ANTI-GRAVITY TECHNOLOGY
9) WEREWOLF
10) TWO—RABBOT AND FRANKETTE

11) GOTH AND STEAMPUNK
12) RABBIT, CLOWN, AND TIGER
13) PRINCESS
14) "I'M #1"
15) RIN
16) SEOUL
17) SAN FRANCISCO AND SEATTLE
18) CHICAGO
19) NEW YORK
20) GUARD